THE NEWSHOUND

Squeak Squeak!

Books by Clara Vulliamy

THE DOG SQUAD: THE NEWSHOUND

The Marshmallow Pie series
in reading order

MARSHMALLOW PIE THE CAT SUPERSTAR

MARSHMALLOW PIE THE CAT SUPERSTAR: ON TV

MARSHMALLOW PIE THE CAT SUPERSTAR: IN HOLLYWOOD

MARSHMALLOW PIE THE CAT SUPERSTAR: ON STAGE

The Dotty Detective series
in reading order

DOTTY DETECTIVE

THE PAW PRINT PUZZLE

THE MIDNIGHT MYSTERY

THE LOST PUPPY

THE BIRTHDAY SURPRISE

THE HOLIDAY MYSTERY

For my brothers, Ed and Tom, with much love xx

First published in the United Kingdom by
HarperCollins *Children's Books* in 2023
HarperCollins *Children's Books* is a division of HarperCollins*Publishers* Ltd
1 London Bridge Street
London SE1 9GF

www.harpercollins.co.uk

HarperCollins*Publishers*
Macken House, 39/40 Mayor Street Upper
Dublin 1, D01 C9W8, Ireland

3

ISBN 978–0–00–856533–6

Clara Vulliamy asserts the moral right to be identified
as the author and illustrator of the work.
A CIP catalogue record for this title is available from the British Library.

Typeset in Aldus LT Std 12.5 pt/21
Printed and bound in the UK using 100% renewable electricity at CPI Group (UK) Ltd

THE NEWSHOUND

CLARA VULLIAMY

HarperCollins *Children's Books*

HOUND
News and reviews!

Chapter One

'WHAT IS GOING ON?'

Mum is standing in the kitchen doorway with a shopping bag in each hand. My little sister, Macy, is peeping out from behind her, mouth wide open like a goldfish.

'What?' I say.

'WHAT. IS. *THIS?*' she says again.

'What's what?' I say as casually as I can manage, intently studying my chocolate biscuit.

But it's no good – I just can't keep it going. Mum is staring –

appalled – at something underneath my chair. There are loud snuffling, grumbling and crumb-licking noises. It's pretty small, our flat. Definitely not enough space to hide a dog.

Okay, so this needs explaining.

I first saw the dog last week, on my way home from school, outside the corner shop. I just assumed his owner was inside, buying something. But the next day I saw him again, this time licking an empty ice-cream wrapper on the ground. Then today he was still there, behind a pile of crates. He came up to me.

'Hello, little one,' I said quietly, and he let me gently stroke his head.

At that moment, a delivery van pulled up on to the pavement and the driver jumped out, opening the side door with a clatter. The sudden loud noise spooked the little dog, who darted away. As he leapt into the road, a motorbike came speeding round the corner.

I dived forward and *just* managed to pull him

back to safety. The motorbike swerved and roared away, the rider shouting angrily.

The dog was trembling.

'You've got to be MUCH more careful!' I said to him, my heart pounding in my chest. 'It's *so* dangerous to run into the road like that!' I looked around. Nobody seemed to be looking after him. He shouldn't be out in the world all on his own, surely?

I finally walked on – *extra* slowly, I admit. Every time I glanced over my shoulder, I saw that the little dog was following me. By the time I reached our front door, he was right by my side, looking up at me. I let myself in, and – I didn't mean it to happen, but I didn't mean it *not* to happen either – the dog came in too.

Chapter Two

'He needs to go back to his own home *right this minute*,' Mum is saying.

'But, Mum, I don't know if he even HAS a home – he doesn't have a collar – and, look, he's *so* thin.'

'Well, there's absolutely no way he can stay here,' says Mum. 'Seriously, NO WAY. The landlord would have a fit. Pets are strictly forbidden.'

We are interrupted by Wes, my brother, shuffling into the kitchen.

He steps over the dog as if he isn't even there, opens the cupboard, takes out a bag of crisps and leaves again without saying a single word. Honestly, what weird stuff happens to your brain when you're a teenager?

'Oh, come *on*, Mum – we CAN'T just throw him out,' I persist. 'He's not safe out there on his own. And I bet he's really cute once you get to know him.'

We all look at the dog, who is searching for more biscuit crumbs. He stops to stare up at us. Mum hesitates for just a fraction of a second, and – YES! I seize the moment.

'He can share with me and Macy,' I say over my shoulder as I hurry him out along the hallway and into our tiny bedroom. 'I'll look after him!'

'Just for one night, you hear?' Mum calls out after me. 'I mean it, Eva – ONE NIGHT!'

My bed is pushed up against Macy's bed. Next to it, I have a small cupboard where I keep all my things. Everywhere else is jam-packed with Macy's toys. There isn't enough room for a wardrobe so I have a row of pegs to hang up my clothes – my trackies, a hoodie with a surfing grizzly bear on it and my precious dark-green baker-boy hat.

I bunch up a blanket to make an improvised bed for the dog. He sniffs it and circles round in it and finally settles down. I give him a gentle belly rub. He has big, dark eyes and a worried face. He's not quite a puppy, but I think he's still young. And he really is wafer-thin . . . That's it! That's what I will call him. Wafer.

Meanwhile, Macy is getting totally on board with the whole Wafer thing. She is sitting on the floor, felt-tip pens spilled out everywhere, drawing lots and lots of pictures of him, surrounded by hearts and flowers. She has a habit of giving a running commentary on everything she's doing.

'First a little bit of yellow, then a little bit of pink . . .'

She also has *three* imaginary friends –

Vera, Chuck and Dave – and chats away to them
constantly. As if it wasn't crowded enough in
here already.

With much exasperated huffing and puffing, Mum goes out and comes back with a packet of dog food, *chicken with spring vegetables.*

'This is the SMALLEST size I could find,' she says firmly to Wafer when we're all having our tea, 'because you're *not* staying.' His bowl is empty again in seconds. I secretly slip him half a sausage roll under the table.

Before bedtime I stay up until after Macy has gone to sleep, Wafer snuggled up close to me on the sofa. I borrow Mum's laptop to browse different dog breeds.

Lurcher . . .
greyhound . . .
terrier . . .
whippet, maybe?

Whippets are small, quick and alert, I read, *and tend to be a little shy and nervous at first.* I look at the photo, and at Wafer's long, slender snout and short, smooth coat. Yes, that's it. He's definitely a whippet.

Then I creep into our room, bringing Wafer with me, and treading – the AGONY – on a piece of Lego. With only a silent *ouch*, I get into my bed, and Wafer gets into his.

I watch him snuffle and fidget until he finally falls asleep.

Who are you, Wafer, and where do you come from?

I can't turn on the light in case it wakes up Macy. Instead, I reach for an old shoebox I keep under the bed. I take out my torch, my extra-special notebook and a double-ended pencil – one end blue, the other red.

There's something else you need to know about me. I'm an ace reporter, brilliant at investigating stories and uncovering secrets. Together with my best friends, we run a newspaper called **THE NEWSHOUND**. So, if there's anybody who can get to the bottom of this mystery, it's us.

Chapter Three

'Get a move on, folks,' says Mum. 'We're going to be late – AS USUAL.'

I finish my cereal and give Wafer the last few morsels of food from the packet, which he hoovers up appreciatively. I think he might like some fresh air too. There's a roof garden at the back of our

flat – well, 'garden' is a bit of an exaggeration: there's an upturned flowerpot to sit on, a washing line and a generator that makes a never-ending buzzing noise like a massive bee. But I love being out here, looking across the rooftops and the railway towards the park in the distance. And it's perfect for Wafer – with the window propped open, he can come and go as much as he likes.

Mum *might* be saying something about sending Wafer away today, but she has a piece of toast clamped between her teeth – brushing Macy's hair with one hand and wiping toothpaste off her sweatshirt with the other – so I *definitely* can't hear her.

I give Wafer a bowl of water and one last scratch behind the ear, then I shove my notebook in my pocket, grab my backpack and it's time to go.

We shout goodbye to Wes, but he has his headphones on and doesn't answer. Then me, Mum and Macy hurtle down four flights of stairs and out of the front door. Mum rushes on ahead to drop Macy off at school before going to work at the Sunny Side Up Community Diner. Mornings are her busiest time, getting ready for the lunchtime rush.

I meet my two friends, who are waiting for me on the corner, and we walk to school together.

Simone and Ash have been my best friends since we were really small. They run **THE NEWSHOUND** with me. I am the main writer, while Simone is BRILLIANT at art, and does all our lettering and illustrations. Ash is the cleverest person in the whole world – they are the newspaper's STAR RESEARCHER.

Yes – they! Ash is non-binary, and doesn't feel like a girl, but doesn't feel like a boy either. So instead of 'he' and 'him' or 'she' and 'her', for Ash we all say 'they' and 'them'. They say it's so much better than being put in a box with the wrong label stuck on the outside. 'I'm just me!' they tell us. Simone made them a cool badge to remind everyone.

they
them

'We've got a new story for **THE NEWSHOUND** to investigate!' I tell them as we walk along. 'And this one is going to be HUGE.'

To be honest, we haven't covered anything nearly as important as this before. We wrote a story about when Orla saw a ghost in the

THE NEW

Top local stories! What's o.

IS OUR SCHOOL
HAUNTED?

playground behind the recycling bins, and another when Vijay won a dance competition. But with Wafer the stakes are *really* high.

HOUND
News and reviews!

First prize for Vijay! page 2

Lost and Found page 5
Are these YOUR gloves?

I tell them both all about Wafer as we walk along. 'I found him outside the shop. He had been there for DAYS and he *nearly* got run over . . .'

'Oh NO!' Ash exclaims.

'It was a really close shave,' I say. 'Then he followed me home, but Mum says he can't stay. We need to find Wafer's owners and return him.'

Although I can't help wishing he doesn't have any, so there's just a *chance* I can keep him.

'It must be amazing to have a dog, even if only for a little while,' says Simone. 'Me and my sisters have been begging for a pet FOR YEARS, but anything hairy makes my dad sneeze and his eyes itchy. He says if we got a dog either him or the dog would have to live in the shed, and he knows it would end up being him!'

Ash has a cat called Frank. 'He's on a diet again,' they tell us. 'We *really* think it's going to work this time.'

We arrive at school, and wander over to join our class at the main door. 'Line up quickly!' says Mr Fuller, our teacher, dunking a digestive into his cup of tea.

Some of the girls are in a huddle, intently looking at something. Turns out it's Amy's birthday party invitations. We don't expect to be invited, which is just as well because we're not.

'You aren't invited,' Max says to us with a smirk.

'Thank you, Captain Obvious,' I mutter under my breath.

'*Newshound* meeting at lunch?' I suggest to Simone and Ash, and they both say YES.

Chapter Four

Me and Ash have school dinners and Simone brings a packed lunch, but we always sit together. The dinner lady I like best is serving today, and gives me extra beans. We call all the people who serve us our lunch 'dinner ladies', not by their names, even Milly's dad who I know for a fact is called Phil.

We rush to finish eating, then I brush away the crumbs with my sleeve and get out my notebook. I look at what I jotted down the night before – mainly a description of Wafer, and a LOT of unanswered questions.

'So,' I say, 'the Wafer story . . . where should we start?'

'We go to the corner shop where you first saw him,' says Ash, 'and do a thorough search of the area.'

'I'll bring my sketchbook and drawing things,' says Simone, checking her pencil case.

'Yes!' I agree. 'And we can ask the shopkeeper too, find out if he saw anything.'

RULE NUMBER ONE: *when you're chasing a story, retrace your steps and start at the very beginning.*

After school, we put on our press passes that Simone made for us and head to the corner shop.

We search everywhere – around the bunches of flowers in buckets, behind the bubblegum vending machine, under the empty crates . . . but find nothing.

We go into the shop. Me and Ash usually do the talking. Simone is a bit shy and prefers to concentrate on drawing in her sketchbook. It's teamwork. We all have our own special talents.

'Do you know anything about a dog that's been hanging around outside recently?' Ash asks the shopkeeper.

'A small, skinny grey dog?' I add. But he shakes his head. 'There are so many people coming in and out, so many dogs waiting at the door. I haven't seen anything unusual.'

'Okay,' I say, 'thank you anyway.'

'A dead end,' says Simone as we walk away.

'Someone must know Wafer,' I say. 'He couldn't have just appeared out of thin air!'

'We need to plan our next move,' says Ash decisively.

RULE NUMBER TWO: *keep digging.*

The minute I get home, I hurry to my bedroom. Wafer is still here, dozing in his blanket bed. I'm VERY glad to see him. So Mum hasn't sent him away – at least not yet. Is that because she is starting to like him, even just a little bit?

He opens one eye, then gets to his feet. At first, he hesitates in the hallway, hearing voices in the kitchen, and hangs back timidly. But when I reassure him – 'Don't worry, Wafer! Everything's fine!' – he follows me in through the door.

Mum is sitting at the kitchen table with Macy, who is doing some cutting and sticking. There's another packet of dog food, again the smallest size.

'We need to find out if Wafer is microchipped,' says Mum, studying something on her phone. 'This is how dogs are identified and reunited with their owners, apparently. We'll find somewhere tomorrow.'

I don't answer straight away. Obviously, it would be great to find out if Wafer belongs to somebody. I had just hoped it wouldn't be quite so soon.

She watches me carefully spooning food into Wafer's bowl.

'Don't let him feel *too* at home,' she adds. 'He won't be staying for long.'

Chapter Five

It happens so fast. Wes puts his ham sandwich on
the worktop and turns away for just a moment . . .

Wafer jumps up, and his jaw clamps round the
bread before he disappears under the kitchen table,
wolfing the whole sandwich down in seconds.

Wes groans. It's too late to make another one, so he'll just have to go without today.

Before school, me and Mum take Wafer to Pet Planet, the local vet and pet-supplies shop, to get him checked to see if he has been microchipped.

'Happy to help!' says the vet, and we follow him into the treatment room.

The vet lifts Wafer up on to the table, all the while chatting away to him cheerfully. 'Don't worry, buddy!' he says. 'This won't hurt a bit!'

He runs the scanner first over Wafer's shoulders, then his body and legs . . . but nothing . . . There's no microchip to be found. No ID pops up on the screen.

'A complete mystery,' says the vet, puzzled. 'No record of him anywhere!'

It's another dead end.

After leaving Pet Planet, there's no time to discuss it further as we both need to hurry.

'Drop by at the diner after school, Eva,' Mum calls out to me. 'I'm working late today and there will be no one at home to look after you.'

In class, we are meant to be doing *quiet reading,* but Mr Fuller has popped out for a minute so the entire room erupts into loud chatting. I use this opportunity to tell Simone and Ash about the visit to Pet Planet.

'So we *still* don't know who Wafer is,' I say, 'or where he came from.'

'What do we do next?' asks Simone.

'I'm busy after school,' I reply. 'I have to go to the diner and wait for Mum.'

'We'll come too,' says Ash. 'Could be a good place to ask around, see if anyone knows Wafer.'

'Good idea!' I say. 'Someone must have seen SOMETHING, surely?'

We are interrupted by Amy, Sumaya and Scarlett at the next table to ours, who are talking about the birthday party. 'There's going to be a karaoke machine!' announces Amy. The other two *ooh* and *ahh* with excitement. They start making plans to go dress shopping together at the weekend.

I must admit the karaoke does sound fun, but shopping for dresses is *not* our idea of a good day out.

Simone rolls her eyes. 'When I went to my cousin's wedding last summer,' she tells us, 'me and my two sisters had to wear identical frilly party dresses in three different sizes, with the same matching hairbands and lacy socks.' She pulls a face. 'I *hated* it!'

Looking down at Simone's black leggings and scuffed baseball boots I just can't imagine her in a frilly dress, and, although I try not to, I start laughing. This sets Ash off chuckling. Simone pretends to be offended, but joins in too. The girls at the next table look over at us, which only makes us laugh more.

We don't worry about what other people think, or want to be the same as everybody else. Besides, it's useful for our reporting – outsiders can see things without being noticed.

Chapter Six

From the street, the diner looks shabby. The paint is flaky and the sign is missing some of its letters. But inside it's warm and cosy and smells *so good*.

We slide into one of the booths, and Mum puts a plate of waffle scraps – the offcuts and misshapes – down on to the faded check tablecloth in front of us, and a bowl of cinnamon sugar to dip them into. YUM.

We look around at the other customers.

'Have you heard anything about a missing dog?' I ask the man in the booth next to ours. 'A whippet – small, grey, worried expression?'

He is mopping up a toddler who has squeezed

broccoli purée through her clenched fists. ''Fraid not!' he says.

Ash goes over to a young woman who is paying her bill at the counter. 'And one for the jar, please,' she says to Mum. I've never understood this because there isn't actually a jar at all. What it means is that you give a little extra, to pay for a coffee or a sandwich for someone else who doesn't have enough money at the moment.

'Do you know anyone who's lost a dog?' Ash asks her.

She smiles, but says, 'Sorry, I don't think so.'

In the corner, an old man is slowly sipping his coffee. I hadn't spotted him at first. It's Mr Brent, a regular at the diner, with his old dog, Lucky, sitting at his feet, her four-leaf clover tag just visible on her collar. They are both a little deaf and cranky. Mum says they've been through a lot together.

'A lost whippet, you say?' asks Mr Brent, turning to us, cupping his hand to his ear.

'YES!' we reply loudly, hurrying over.

'I *think* there was a dodgy local whippet breeder in the news a while back,' he tells us. 'Got into trouble when they were found to be selling puppies illegally . . .'

I get a funny feeling in my stomach that tells me we might be on to something.

'What happened to the puppies?' I ask.

'Oh, I don't remember . . .' he answers, shaking his head.

'This could be important!' says Ash, and we pack up to leave.

'Might this be where Wafer came from?' asks Simone.

'I don't know,' I reply. 'But it's a lead!'

The next day at morning break, we head straight to the school library. Our librarian (Miss Kapoor, but she says we can call her Meera) lets us spend as much time in here as we like. She is **THE NEWSHOUND**'s BIGGEST supporter.

Also, she often has treats. Today she takes a Tupperware box out from her desk and gives us each a square of rose-and-pistachio shortbread.

'AMAZING,' says Simone indistinctly, mouth very full.

readers
writers
Everyone is
artists
welcome
dreamers
our library!
thinkers
explorers

Then we log on to the internet, and begin our search. It's a needle in a haystack – there are SO MANY puppy stories in the local news:

Puppy-training classes in the park, starting soon . . .

Dalmation puppies needed for a new show at the Theatre Grande . . .

Downward Dog – yoga classes for you and your puppy . . .

I put my hair up into a topknot and absent-mindedly stick a pencil through it, which is something I do when I am *really* concentrating.

And then . . .

Simone spots it first. 'This is it!'

WHIPPET PUPPY BREEDER FORCED TO CLOSE DOWN!

Local animal protection officers have discovered an unlicensed breeder selling whippet puppies illegally. The puppies were being handed over to buyers in a car park, rather than at a registered address, in exchange for large sums of money. They had been born into a noisy, overcrowded environment and separated from their mother when they were still too young.

'That's *terrible*!' I burst out.

'We MUST write about this in **THE NEWSHOUND**,' says Ash.

We read on . . .

The breeder has now been ordered to close down their business. Unfortunately, because they were sold without any paperwork and the puppies weren't microchipped, it is impossible to establish where the puppies are now.

'So this *could* be where Wafer came from!' Simone says.

'But there's no way to be sure,' Ash replies.

I ask Meera to print out the newspaper article for us anyway. I fold it up and put it in my notebook.

RULE NUMBER THREE: *keep track of every detail, however small. You never know what might be important.*

Chapter Seven

On my way home from school, I buy a packet of dog chews for Wafer from Pet Planet – *sizzling steak* flavour. When I get in, I find him with Macy and Mum in the kitchen. He has dragged his blanket in and curled up under the table. He's getting much more confident and trusting with us all now.

'Hey, Wafer!' I say, giving him a couple of chews. His tail is a blur of waggy joy.

After tea, I decide that Wafer needs a BATH.

I'm not sure if Wafer loves or hates this idea, but as soon as he's in the water he goes crazy with excitement. He knocks over a bottle of shampoo, which drips steadily into the water. By now, I'm wrestling with a REALLY soapy dog.

I let go of the shower attachment, which has a
life of its own. It is wriggling like a snake, a
fountain of water making a huge puddle on the
floor. Wafer takes a big lick of the soap, and his
snout disappears under a cloud of
bubbles.

I hurry him out and quickly mop up before Mum sees.

Gently, I dry Wafer and wrap him in his blanket on the sofa like a burrito. Mum comes in with a bowl of popcorn and sits down with us, and we start watching a film together. We often have a movie night on Fridays, although she almost always falls asleep a few minutes in,

and wakes up at the end saying, 'That was *lovely*!'

I notice Mum absent-mindedly giving Wafer a couple of pieces of popcorn, and a little pat on the top of his soft, silky head. I think she's warming to him.

Wafer LOVES watching TV. He'll watch absolutely anything, even more than my nan, and that's *really* saying something.

But it's never, EVER peaceful for long in this place. Here comes Macy, way past her bedtime, loudly and proudly announcing her new project: a mobile nail salon. She has been rummaging in the bathroom cupboard and has filled a carrier bag with Mum's nearly empty bottles of nail varnish and some cotton wool balls.

'I'm too tired to argue,' says Mum, lying back on the sofa, taking off her socks and closing her eyes. By the time she opens them again, her entire toes are a mess of sticky, glittery colour.

'That will be fifty p!' Macy tells her.

'Well, I admire your business spirit,' Mum replies, reaching for her bag and giving her the money. 'Keep it up and I can quit my job.'

She says that, but I know she would *never* give up the diner.

I manage to get out of having my nails done, but Macy persuades Wes to be her next customer.

'Three pounds!' she tells him brightly. He gives her 20p.

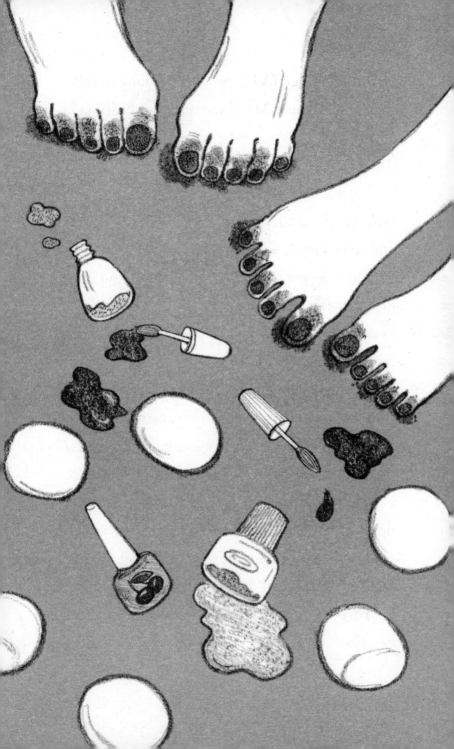

Chapter Eight

Wafer hears the postman first and jumps to his feet on full alert.

It's a parcel for Mum. She has bought Wafer a lead, and a fleecy coat in a lovely pink and orange check.

'Not that he's staying, *obviously*,' she tells us.

Which sets me thinking . . . perhaps Wafer has been spending too much time indoors and is turning into a couch potato. I'm meeting Simone and Ash at the park this morning, so why doesn't he come with me? 'I'm taking Wafer out for some exercise!' I tell Mum.

Simone and Ash are waiting for us by the park
gate when we get there. They both crouch down to
say hello to Wafer.

'He looks very cosy in his coat,' Ash says.

'And so stylish!' Simone adds.

'It's new,' I tell them. 'Mum bought it for him. I
think she likes him more than she's letting on.'

We head past the playground and walk round the duck pond. In the wooded area, I let Wafer off the lead and he tears off into the trees, running in a huge circle before coming back to us. Boy, whippets can go FAST.

While Wafer goes crazy
chasing a leaf, we sit on a bench
and Ash takes a bag of mixed
chocolates from their pocket.

'Let's play the chocolate-
guessing game,' they say. This is
one of our favourites – a chance

to show off our INVESTIGATIVE SKILLS.

Simone goes first.

'Smooth and round . . . orange?' she guesses, popping a chocolate into her mouth. 'YES!'

Now it's my turn.

'Small and oval . . . I'm guessing toffee?' But no, ugh, it's raisin.

Then Ash.

'Smooth and round again . . . coffee this time? YES.'

I insist on another go to make up for my terrible mistake and guess the malted-crisp chocolate RIGHT. Let me tell you, we are *professionally trained* for this game.

After a while, we move on, Wafer insisting on bringing an extra-precious stick with him. As we walk round the other side of the pond and back towards the gate, we are too busy chatting to spot the danger immediately. Then I look up and see a familiar figure walking down the path towards us . . .

'It's our LANDLORD!' I gasp.

Quick as a flash, we duck behind the nearest bushes, bringing Wafer with us. I hardly dare breathe, and Simone has her hand clamped over her mouth. Wafer, thank goodness, is quiet, distracted by his stick. We don't move a muscle as I sense the landlord getting nearer . . . and I glimpse his legs through the leaves, passing very close by . . . until finally he walks on and disappears round the corner.

When the coast is clear and we emerge on to the path again, I burst out laughing.

'HA! See?' I say. 'It was SO easy to hide from him!'

'Almost *too* easy!' Ash says, laughing too.

Simone is a little more flustered at first, but soon relaxes and joins in. Feeling happy and very sure of ourselves, we make our way to the gate, before going our separate ways home.

Mum is doing the diner's accounts at the kitchen table, surrounded by piles of bills and receipts, and Macy is having a tea party with her imaginary friends. I take Wafer into the front room.

After a good run, it seems that Wafer is happy to snooze on the sofa for the rest of the day. I put my feet up too. *We managed the encounter with the landlord in the park so brilliantly*, I think to myself. It's been easy so far to keep Wafer hidden. And it looks like nobody knows anything about him, either.

Although I should never forget **RULE NUMBER FOUR**: *don't get complacent; don't take your eye off the ball . . .*

I can't help wondering . . . Could we keep Wafer hidden *forever*?

Chapter Nine

A few days go past. I'm getting used to having Wafer around. We hang out together in the flat, and we go to the park again. This time there's no sign of the landlord. Mum buys more *chicken with spring vegetables* dog food, in medium size.

I go to the school library with Ash and Simone every breaktime, and we make a start on our story for **THE NEWSHOUND**. Me and Ash research more about illegal puppy breeders, while Simone designs the pages and finds the right pictures.

In the afternoons when I get back from school, I often find Wafer out on the roof garden, dozing in the sunshine. I go out there with him, and sit on the upturned flowerpot, doing my homework. Sometimes he whimpers and trembles, as if he's having a bad dream. I gently stroke his bony head, his soft ears, his warm, velvety back, until he quietens and goes back to sleep.

Wafer has settled in really well. Everything feels so right. What could possibly go wrong?

It's early morning, and I wake with a start. I can hear the landlord's voice in the kitchen. 'I've come over to sort out that broken light switch,' he is saying to Mum.

I look at Wafer's bed. It's empty. With my stomach turning over in panic, I tear down the hallway and burst into the kitchen. The landlord looks up from his toolbox, startled.

'Don't mind Eva,' says Mum airily. 'She just wants to see what you're doing – she's very keen to be an electrician when she grows up!' She gives me a meaningful look.

I switch on *reporter mode*, and scan the room. No sign of Wafer. His bowl isn't on the floor – it must be in the dishwasher. GOOD. Mum is standing with her back to the roof-garden window. This could be important. I look past her and see, poking out from behind the generator, a snout, a paw, a closed eye: it's Wafer, fast asleep in his favourite spot.

The landlord is tinkering with the light switch for what feels like a hundred years. I see Wafer sit up, alert to the presence of someone he doesn't know in the flat . . . then he gets to his feet and starts walking towards us. I hurry over to stand squashed up next to Mum, blocking the view. We must look very strange. I put on my best 'fascinated by DIY' face.

The landlord finishes his work, packs away his tools, and looks over at us to say goodbye.

Come on, come on – *just LEAVE!* I am screaming inside my head.

Now he is looking over our shoulders, frowning. Wafer is pressing his nose up against the glass behind us.

'And who is THAT?' demands the landlord.

'His name is Wafer,' I manage to answer, 'and he has nowhere else to go.'

'But he's not staying,' Mum adds quickly.

'NO PETS!' the landlord says firmly. 'Those are the rules! He must leave IMMEDIATELY.'

I feel sick. When he sees how devastated I am, the landlord relents, but only a little . . .

'I'll give you until after the weekend,' he says. 'That's three days. But then he must go.'

Once the landlord has left, I let Wafer in and give him a hug.

'We *must* find out where Wafer comes from and take him back,' says Mum, 'and SOON.' She tries not to let it show, but I can tell she is sad about it.

I don't say anything about our investigations for **THE NEWSHOUND**. **RULE NUMBER FIVE**: *keep your story under your hat until you have ALL THE FACTS.*

But it's getting urgent. Wafer needs our help.

We *must* keep trying. I kneel down and look into his trusting little face.

'We have THREE DAYS to find your owner,' I say to him. 'Or to prove *beyond doubt* that you don't have one and to find a way to keep you. I haven't given up hope yet!'

Chapter Ten

Only three days! What can we do? An idea pops into my head . . .

POSTERS! We could put them up all around town. Maybe *someone* will recognise Wafer and come forward to claim him.

I'll need to take a photo of Wafer – and quickly, because I leave for school in a minute. This isn't easy as he will NOT keep still. First, he is too far away, then he is too close . . .

One minute he's looking for something under the sofa and only shows his bottom, the next he's pulling his blanket up over himself and only shows his feet. FINALLY, I get a good picture.

As we line up in the school playground, I tell Ash and Simone the bad news: the landlord has discovered Wafer and given us an ultimatum.

'We need to step up our efforts to find his owner!' I say. 'I thought we could make posters that say FOUND DOG, with Wafer's picture?'

'Great plan,' says Ash. 'Let's get straight on it today.'

'I can design them,' says Simone. 'Library, lunchtime?'

Amy and her friends are excitedly chatting about her party again. 'We're going to have a chocolate fountain,' Amy says, 'and a special spa and pedicure!'

'A chocolate fountain sounds good,' Ash says to us, a little dejectedly.

'It does,' I agree. 'And the spa. Oh well. For a pedicure there's always Macy's mobile nail salon – not sure it's *quite* as good, though.'

The morning seems to drag on *forever* . . .

But, at last, here we are in the library, getting our posters made.

'These look great!' says Meera. She sets
them printing, and lends us some tape from her
stationery drawer. In exchange, she gives us a box
of books to put away, and asks us to straighten up
the chairs. She often has jobs for us to do, which is
fair enough.

After school, we put the posters up everywhere
we can think of – one on the notice board in the
playground, two at the park gate . . .

The owner of the corner shop lets us put one
in their window, and the receptionist at Pet Planet
does too.

Finally, we arrive at the diner. Mum looks up
from hammering a nail into a wonky table leg, and
smiles at us through the window. 'Perfect!' she
says, seeing our posters. 'I'll take as many as you
can find room for, please!' So we put three posters
up in the window, two on the counter and two on
the door.

FOUND DOG!

Grey whippet, a bit nervous and shy, but
very friendly when you get to know him.
No collar or microchip. Do you know this dog?
Please leave a message for us at
the Community Diner on the high street.

Back at home, I find Wafer snoozing on the sofa. 'Budge up!' I say to him. He's only small, but always finds a way to take up *maximum* space. He lays his head on my lap. I get out my notebook, and use my special reporter's double-ended red and blue pencil: blue for proper leads, red for dead ends. Now the posters are up all over town, we can't just sit and wait for something to happen. We need to keep pressing on with the next steps.

I glance up at a framed picture on the wall above the TV. It's *Eva's News*, the first newspaper I ever made, many years ago. The headline story is 'I SAW A HEDGEHOG', with a funny childish drawing. I've always wanted to be a reporter, ever since I was really small. I used to interview passers-by with a skipping-rope handle, pretending it was a microphone, asking them their favourite colour or what they'd had for breakfast. You know, the Really BIG Questions.

I think about what a long time I've been doing

this job, working hard on my skills to become a really good reporter. And with Ash and Simone alongside me, we make a great team. If anyone can find out the truth and tell this story, it's **THE NEWSHOUND**. We just need to focus and keep going.

RULE NUMBER SIX: *a good reporter is like a dog with a bone. Hold on tight and never give up.*

But my thoughts are interrupted by a hullabaloo. Wafer, always alert, jumps up and runs into the kitchen. He's noticed that the toast for Macy's boiled egg is burning, and barks loudly until Mum rushes to the rescue.

Chapter Eleven

We had arranged to meet at the park on Saturday morning for an emergency *Newshound* meeting.

'Only two days left!' I say to Ash and Simone when I arrive. 'We're running out of time!'

'Where should we be looking next?' asks Simone.

We sit in silence for a bit.

'The trail went cold after the illegal-breeder story,' says Ash, 'but those puppies must have gone to new homes . . . What about one of those doggy day-care centres, who look after people's dogs while they're at work? There's one on the high street – WAGS AND WHISKERS. They might know something. Shall we interview them?'

We all agree that this is a fantastic idea. No time to waste: we put on our press passes, grab our notebooks and jump to our feet.

We arrive at WAGS AND WHISKERS just as two of the staff are coming back from taking the dogs for a walk. I have NEVER SEEN so many dogs of different shapes and sizes.

'Hi!' he says cheerfully. 'I'm Sam. How can I help?'

'We'd like to interview you for our newspaper, **THE NEWSHOUND**,' I say. 'Can you spare a few minutes?'

'Sure!' he replies. 'Have a seat – if you can find one. We are CRAZILY busy at the moment!' Almost every chair has a dog sitting on it, or is piled high with a jumble of pet toys, blankets and boxes.

We tell him about Wafer, and our urgent need to find his owner, if he even has one.

'Has anyone brought in a whippet for you to look after?' I ask hopefully.

'Sadly not,' Sam answers. 'There hasn't been a whippet here for ages.'

'We think Wafer might have something to do with

the illegal whippet breeder in the news recently,' says Ash, 'although we can't be sure.'

'Ah yes, I remember that story,' says Sam. 'Lots of people are buying puppies these days, and not always from respectable breeders. But having a pet is a *big* responsibility. Some people just don't think it through. After a while, they find that they can't, or don't want to, look after them any more.'

'What happens to the dogs then?' asks Ash.

'Lots of unwanted dogs are handed in to animal-rescue shelters,' Sam tells us, 'who then try to rehome them. Some people pretend that their own dogs are strays, that they found them on the streets – too embarrassed to tell the truth, I suppose.'

We are interrupted by a commotion of barking and excitement, because it's dinnertime for the dogs. So we thank Sam for his help, gather up our things and leave.

Ash needs to rush off because they are going on a bike ride with their dad, so for a treat me and

Simone go to the diner to share a milkshake. We study the menu for AGES, even though we know we are having Strawberries and Cream because we've been discussing it *all week*.

While we sip our drink through two straws, we mull over the interview at WAGS AND WHISKERS.

'It was sad to hear about all those unwanted dogs,' says Simone.

'Yes, really awful,' I agree. 'Getting a pet isn't like buying a car or a new phone or a handbag! It's really good that we're covering this in **THE NEWSHOUND**.'

I think about Wafer and how desperately I wish I could keep him. If he belonged to me, I wouldn't give him up for *anything*!

'No response to our posters so far,' Simone says.

'Which is really disappointing, obviously,' I answer.

But I can't help feeling a *tiny* bit pleased too.

Chapter Twelve

It's Sunday, our last day to get to the bottom of Wafer's story. Mum says that if we haven't found his owner by the end of the weekend, he will have to go to a dogs' home. It dawns on me that I would probably never see him again.

I want to spring into action RIGHT NOW, but the phone rings. It's Mum's assistant Harry from the diner, who does the weekend shifts.

'Have you checked the fuse box?' Mum is saying. Then she hangs up with a sigh. 'I've got to go out for a bit,' she tells me. 'Will you entertain Macy while I'm gone? Wes is here, but he's busy with his college project.'

Macy wants to play schools. She is the teacher, and me and her imaginary friends are the pupils. We are each given paper and pens.

'Write down what I am thinking!' she commands.

I give it a go, but it's practically impossible.

At the end of the lesson, she collects the papers, saying, 'No, no – that wasn't it at all.' She shakes her head sorrowfully. 'I'm not cross, just VERY DISAPPOINTED.' We all get a really low mark.

I jump up the second Mum gets back.

'I'm going out to see Simone and Ash,' I tell her.

'Okay,' she says, 'see you later.'

I call by for Simone on the way, and we arrive at Ash's house together.

'Eva! Simone!' says Ash's dad, opening the front door. 'Come in, come in!'

We follow him into the kitchen. Their cat, Frank, is there, tucking into an enormous plate of tuna chunks. So much for his diet.

Ash shrugs with an apologetic smile. 'What can we do?' they say. 'He's a big, hungry boy!'

'Will you stay for lunch?' their dad asks. 'I've made far too much for just us two.'

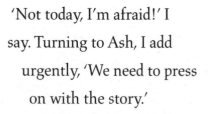

'Not today, I'm afraid!' I say. Turning to Ash, I add urgently, 'We need to press on with the story.'

We look through our notes, discussing our next move.

'Sam at WAGS AND WHISKERS told us that unwanted dogs are sometimes left at an animal-rescue shelter,' Simone reminds us.

'Then that's where we should look next!' I reply.

Ash asks their dad if we can borrow his laptop, and we begin our search for all the animal-rescue shelters in the area. There are *hundreds* of pets up for adoption, page after page of descriptions to trawl through.

'Affectionate old girl,' we read, 'in need of a quiet, peaceful home away from the hustle and bustle. Owner sadly died . . .'

'Cheeky twins, very playful. Adore each other and must be rehomed together . . .'

At Happy Tails Rescue, one in particular catches our eye:

'A sweet-natured and sensitive boy who's not had the best start in life. Loves a cuddle. Reason for arrival: no longer wanted.'

And there's a photo . . .

It's Wafer.

So now we know for certain: Wafer has no owners, no family. He had been waiting at Happy Tails Rescue for someone to adopt him and give him a home. That's where he must have escaped from.

We sit quietly for a few minutes, feeling very downhearted. At the thought of him going back to the shelter, I am even more desperate to keep him. And I'm

CERTAIN that Mum would love him to stay too. But the landlord's three days are nearly up, and he's made it absolutely clear: pets are strictly forbidden – Wafer must go.

I trudge slowly home, and tell Mum about our discovery.

'You did really well to find out where Wafer came from,' she says, and she gives me a hug. 'I think we should call Happy Tails now. Shall I do it, or will you?'

'I'll do it,' I say, and I pick up the phone.

The friendly woman who answers confirms that Wafer is indeed one of their residents, and provides the last missing piece of his story.

'He was abandoned on our doorstep a little while back,' she tells me. 'Such a nervous little chap. It's sad when this happens, but we don't judge people. You never know what problems they might be having in their lives. We just want to help.'

'I'm amazed nobody adopted him from you straight away!' I say.

'Us too!' she replies. 'But because he was so shy and timid, when visitors came to choose a dog to take home, he would hide from view.'

'I found him outside

the corner shop,' I tell her. 'How did he end up there?'

'He ran away from us last week, on fireworks night. The loud noises frightened him, just as a back door had been left open for a moment, and he bolted. We've been very worried. We are SO grateful to you for finding him and keeping him safe all this time.'

It is all arranged. We will deliver him back to Happy Tails in the morning.

Chapter Thirteen

I wake early, remembering with a huge wave of sadness that Wafer is leaving today. I pack up his few possessions – his fleecy pink-and-orange check coat, his lead and a packet of his favourite dog chews, *sizzling steak* flavour. I look at his empty bed next to mine and only just manage not to cry. I'm going to miss him SO MUCH.

Macy tries to comfort me by saying that I can look at *and even touch* her special collection of plastic ponies. I appreciate the gesture, but I still feel sad.

The doorbell rings – it's Ash and Simone, who have unexpectedly arrived to support me. It's really kind of them. Wafer rushes excitedly to greet them both, assuming that we are all going to the park together.

'We will *all* miss Wafer,' says Ash.

'We shall never forget him,' adds Simone.

It's time to go. We leave the flat together –
Mum and Macy, me, Ash and Simone, and Wafer.
At the bottom of the stairway, we bump into the
landlord, who is changing a lightbulb in the hall.

But Wafer is agitated – barking and whining,
running back up the stairs, looking at the ceiling
and then returning, as if urging us to follow.

Now he is tugging at the landlord's belt . . .

'Hey, what's up?' the landlord asks him,
puzzled.

'He probably just wants to go back to the flat,'
guesses Mum.

But I'm not so sure. I think that Wafer has
spotted something, and I trust him.

RULE NUMBER SEVEN: *always,* always *listen to
your instincts.*

I follow Wafer back up the stairs a little way.
Then I see what he has seen, and has been trying
to draw our attention to: a spreading dark, wet
shape on the ceiling above . . . a drip, drip, drip,
then a splash, splash, splash . . .

'Oh NO!' the landlord exclaims. 'It's a
FLOOD!' He hurtles into action, grabs his
toolbox and rushes down into the basement.

We wait on tenterhooks for a few moments until he reappears and then tears off again, this time up the stairs.

He returns, wiping his forehead with his sleeve and looking greatly relieved. 'I've turned the water off,' he tells us. 'There was an overflowing bath in one of the top flats. It could have caused MASSIVE damage to the whole building!'

Is this our big chance? The moment we have so desperately been waiting for?

But to my huge surprise, me, Eva, *never without an opinion, will say anything to anybody*, can't find the words. They seem to be stuck in my throat and I fall silent. I am so glad my friends are here.

'Wafer saved the day!' says Ash directly to the landlord.

'What a hero!' agrees Simone, loud and clear, overcoming her shyness like an absolute superstar.

'And what an *excellent* watchdog!' Mum says in her most persuasive voice, mainly used for getting us to help put out the bins or empty the dishwasher. 'See how useful it is to have the keen eyes and ears of a dog in the building?'

Macy is nodding in agreement, so much you'd think her head would fall off.

Our neighbours Josie and Beth, hearing the rumpus, come out too and immediately join in.

'Ooh, YES!' says Beth. 'We'd love to have a dog living here. It would make it really homely!'

But the landlord doesn't say anything. He
packs up his tools and loads them into the back of
his car. He opens the driver's door, about to leave.
It all feels hopeless, impossible.

He hesitates, looking back at Wafer. Timidly half
hiding behind my legs, Wafer looks back at him.

I can hardly breathe.
Will he, won't he, change his mind?

Chapter Fourteen

The landlord chuckles to himself, shaking his head.

'I can see I'm totally outnumbered here,' he says. 'Okay. Wafer can stay.'

I wouldn't have believed my ears if Ash and Simone weren't cheering and jumping up and down with joy. The happiness inside me bursts out of my chest in a huge

'WOO HOOOOOOO!'.

I scoop Wafer into my arms and give him the *biggest* hug. 'You did it, Wafer – you did it!'

'You did it together,' says Mum, all smiles, looking at me, Ash and Simone.

Mum phones the people at Happy Tails Rescue, who readily agree to our adoption of Wafer.

They will do a home visit later today, and bring the paperwork for Mum to sign.

'And now you three better make a run for it,' Mum says to us. 'You're already VERY late for school – I'll call the office and explain.'

While we're having our lunch, me, Ash and Simone talk about the amazing events of the morning.

'We could certainly use Wafer's skills on **THE NEWSHOUND**,' says Ash admiringly. 'He is one very smart dog!'

'Yes, he is!' I agree. 'And not just about the flood this morning. There have been other little things along the way too – he always hears the postman first, and another time he noticed when the toast was burning. He's very alert to everything that's going on. He will make an ACE investigative reporter, just like us.'

'A brilliant addition to our team,' says Simone. 'I will make him his very own press pass!'

When we've finished eating, we make a beeline for the library. Now that we have the final missing pieces, we're keen to finish writing up the story for **THE NEWSHOUND** as soon as possible.

THE NEW

Top local stories! What's

MEET WAFER!
THE NEW ADDITION TO
THE NEWSHOUND TEAM!

SHOUND
☆ News and reviews!

EXCLUSIVE!
The do's and don'ts of
getting a puppy page 4

All about Happy Tails
Animal Rescue Shelter
page 7

HAPPY
TAILS

MEET WAFER!
THE NEW ADDITION TO
THE NEWSHOUND TEAM!

Wafer used his incredible skills this week to raise the alarm over what could have been a disastrous flood, after a bath was left to overflow in a block of flats. He is a whippet, a breed known for their speed, alertness and quick reactions. Whippets are also famous for their stealth moves such as counter-surfing – keep an eye on your sandwich or they'll snatch it in seconds!

It's possible that Wafer came from an illegal breeder, but we can't be certain. If you are buying a dog, it's REALLY important to go to a licensed breeder who will make sure the puppies they are selling are happy, healthy and microchipped, and that they stay with their mums until they are old enough to leave.

Remember, dogs are for life, not just to buy on a whim without thinking about it very carefully!

Or you can visit an animal-rescue shelter, who look after unwanted pets while they are waiting for a new owner to adopt them. Because every dog, like Wafer, deserves a chance for a loving forever home.

Meera looks over our shoulder. 'Best edition of **_THE NEWSHOUND_** yet,' she says proudly. 'A triumph! Ready to go to print?'

'Ready!' we all answer together.

As the printer clicks, bleeps and whirrs into action, Meera takes a bag of fresh apricots from her desk and offers us each one.

'So,' she says, 'I see **THE NEWSHOUND** has its very own REAL DOG on the squad now!'

'THE DOG SQUAD!' I say, laughing. 'That's who we are now!'

Chapter Fifteen

The guests are arriving at our post-publication party at the diner. We've been busy all day, helping Mum prepare the drinks and snacks and putting up decorations. We make a display next to the door with copies piled high of **THE NEWSHOUND**, so everybody can take one. We've already left some at Pet Planet and WAGS AND WHISKERS, who are both keen to offer them to their customers.

I'm celebrating by wearing my favourite clothes – my hoodie with a surfing grizzly bear on it, and my dark-green baker-boy hat. Wafer has a new bandana, which Simone made for him, pink and orange to match his coat.

Everyone is here – Ash's dad, Simone's parents
and her two sisters, our neighbours Josie and
Beth . . .

'We can always take Wafer for a walk if you're
busy,' says Josie. 'Just let us know!'

Mr Brent arrives, with his old dog, Lucky. 'Well,
I am very pleased it all worked out,' he
says when we remind him that it was
his top tip that gave us the lead.

Even Wes turns up. 'Cool!'
he says, seeing what we've
achieved, which is frankly
astounding as it's the first
word I've heard him say for
WEEKS.

But the biggest surprise

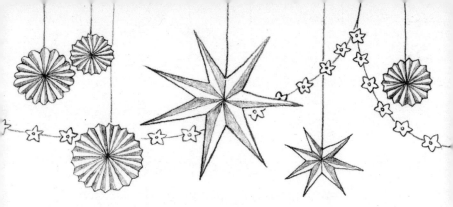

is when Amy, of all people, drops by.

'I just wanted to say well done,' she tells us.
'And, by the way,' she adds, shyly scuffing the
toe of her shoe against the floor, 'I didn't ask you
to my party because I didn't think you'd want to
come . . . but you can come if you want to.'

We are almost too amazed to answer, then Ash
manages to say, 'Yes, please. We'd really like that.'

'We'll have to buy you a frilly dress,' I say to
Simone when Amy's gone, and she shoves me
jokingly on the shoulder.

'So,' says Ash, '*Newshound* meeting tomorrow?
Start making plans for our next story?'

'YES!' I reply.

'Absolutely!' Simone agrees.

Back at home, Macy is supervising the leftover food from the party, heaped up on the kitchen table. She is having one of her long, involved conversations entirely with herself.

'Macy,' says Macy, 'would you like this last piece of cake?'

I roll my eyes.

'Yes, Macy,' Macy carries on, 'I WOULD!'

Mum is tired and puts her feet up. Wes has disappeared into his room, as usual.

I give Wafer a little piece of chicken even though it's not his dinnertime.

'I SAW THAT,' calls Mum from the front room, through two closed doors. *How can she do this?* It must be a Mum Thing.

I take Wafer out on to the roof garden for a little fresh air before bed. I sit on the upturned flowerpot, and watch him snuffling around in the weeds. He finds an old clothes peg and seems very thrilled with it, playing with it over and over in his paws and giving it a chew.

I think about how forgiving he is, after being passed from place to place, trusting humans again after everything he's been through.

'This is your home now, Wafer,' I say to him.

On hearing his name, Wafer looks over and wags his tail. He knows who he is, and that he belongs with us. We are his forever found family.

And I think about what it takes to be a good reporter too. It's partly about uncovering the facts, but it's so much more than that. We are telling the world the real-life stories they need to hear. Most of all, it's about doing the right thing.

I am so excited for the Dog Squad's next adventure!

Check out more of
Clara's books...

Dotty Detective

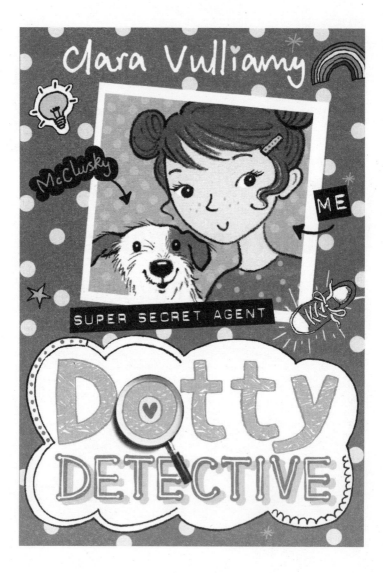

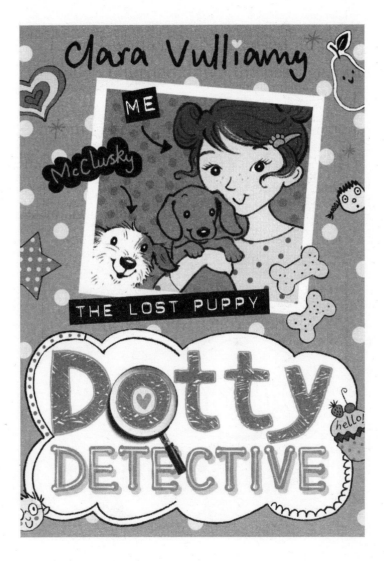

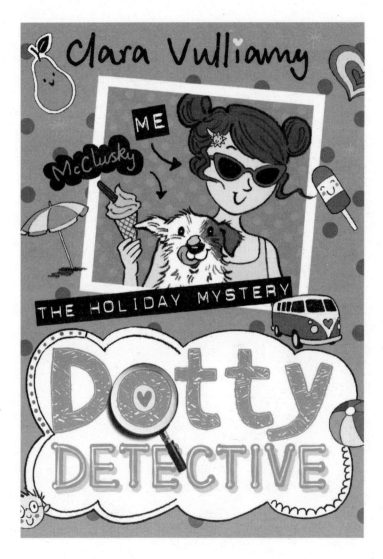

Marshmallow Pie
the Cat Superstar

Marshmallow Pie the Cat Superstar in Hollywood

Clara Vulliamy

Marshmallow Pie the Cat Superstar On Stage

Clara Vulliamy